CORKY

By
PATRICIA SCARRY

Illustrated by
IRMA WILDE

GOLDEN PRESS
Western Publishing Company, Inc.
Racine, Wisconsin

To Lovable Corky Goit

Fifth Printing, 1976

© Copyright 1962 by Western Publishing Company, Inc.
All rights reserved. Produced in U.S.A.

Corky was a big, black, friendly dog.
He lived with a little boy.

Corky loved to carry things in his mouth.
The little boy threw a stick into the sea.
In went Corky, to fetch the stick.

Then Corky raced up the beach with the stick in his mouth.

"Oh, that Corky!" cried the people on the beach, as the sand flew onto their beach towels.

One day the little boy took Corky to the pond in the park.

And Corky jumped in after the toy sailboats.

"No Corky!" said the little boy. "Put that boat back!"

When the little boy played ball,
Corky ran after the ball.

Proudly Corky carried the ball to home plate. "No Corky! Drop the ball! No, no!" everyone wailed.

Corky loved everybody.

He liked to bring them presents.

One morning Mrs. Cooper was having break-
fast in her garden.

Corky brought her a pretty green garden snake
and dropped it on her foot.

"Eeeeek!" shrieked Mrs. Cooper.

The only person Corky didn't like was the little boy's teddy bear.

That bear never let Corky be alone with his little boy for one minute. He rode with him in his kiddy car while Corky had to run behind.

And when the little boy took his nap, that rag bear slept on the pillow beside him.

Poor Corky had to sleep under the bed.

Once, Corky found the bear alone. He took him out to the garbage can.

But the little boy found him and said, "Oh you naughty dog!"

Poor Corky.

One day Corky was at the beach chasing beach balls.

"Please take your dog home," said the lifeguard.

The little boy left Teddy Bear at the water's edge to guard a sand castle.

Later on, nobody could remember where Teddy Bear was.

He didn't turn up for supper.

Everybody looked.

All the neighbors looked.

And at bedtime there was no bear to take to bed.

The little boy cried.

Corky cried too. He sat in the garden and howled.

He howled until Mr. Cooper next door threw a shoe out of the window.

Corky caught the shoe in his mouth and
brought it back to Mr. Cooper's door.
He scratched and scratched.
But Mr. Cooper wouldn't open the door.
He just shouted, "Corky, go home!"

Sadly, Corky went down to the beach.
The tide had washed the castles out to sea.
To cheer himself up, Corky chased some seagulls.

This was a game the gulls enjoyed too. A playful old seagull, who was Corky's friend, dropped a clam on his nose.

Then he fluttered to the sea wall and waited for Corky to chase him.

Corky raced along the rocks. And the gull swooped. Corky skidded to the end of the rocks. SPLASH! Into the water he fell.

He came up sneezing. And mad. Then his nose bumped something soft.

Why, it was the lost teddy bear!
Corky raced for home with the wet bear in his
mouth.
He scratched and scratched on the door.
He whined. He howled!

At last the little boy's daddy came to the door.
He looked very cross.

But when Corky dropped the wet bear onto
his slipper, oh, how he smiled!

Everyone was so happy to have Bear back
home!

The little boy hugged his bear. He gave Corky
a warm hug and a kiss, too, and took him right
up to his bed.

There Corky slept, all wet and sandy, his tail thumping with happiness.

After that Corky and Bear were friends. And everyone called Corky a Hero!